I0628003

Dead Ball Situation
Sporting Pride #4
Charity Parkerson

Punk & Sissy Publications

Copyright

—Warning: This book is intended for readers over the age of 18. Some of my books contain allusions to past abuse and trauma.

Contents

Introduction

*BANDIT IS HIS BOSS'S **best friend**. Sacha can't risk his job over some pointless desire. Except Sacha isn't so sure it's hopeless any longer.*

For nearly six years, Sacha has worked for *the* wedding planner for the stars. Since his boss had a health scare, Sacha has more on his plate than ever before. He's also finding himself in Baylor's best friend's company more and more often. It's a position he loves and hates. If anything happened between them and went south, Sacha would be out of work and on the street. He's not a hundred percent sure he cares anymore.

Since the first time Bandit met Sacha, he's been more than interested. Unfortunately, the guy doesn't seem to notice Bandit at all. Bandit knows if he could get Sacha to see him as more than Baylor's best friend, he might have a shot. Surely that's all that stands between them. What else could be? Their chances can't be dead before they even start. Bandit is way too persistent for that.

Dead Ball Situation is the fourth book in Charity Parkerson's Sporting Pride series. These are sports-related romances, following men who find love while navigating high-profile careers. These are best enjoyed when read in order.

Chapter One

Chapter One

THE WAY COUNTLESS GROWN people bounced inside a bouncy house while others played various lawn games blew Bandit's mind. It also warmed his heart. Baylor deserved this happy wedding that showed exactly how much joy Chipper would bring to his life. Baylor had been his best friend since he was too young to recall. Hell, Bandit's parents were here. Since they had traveled over three thousand miles just to watch Baylor marry, that showed exactly how deeply entrenched Baylor was in his life. It had always been the two of them. Bandit prayed that didn't change.

While this wasn't the first time Bandit had watched Baylor marry, it was still different. The first time, Baylor had married one of Bandit's teammates. That had kept him close. Now, while Bandit still played pro soccer for New England, Baylor would live in California with the larger-than-life MMA champion he had married. Bandit had a bad feeling this time would be the time he never really saw Baylor any longer. The thought had him fighting the urge to massage his chest. Bandit knew a lot of people. He had a lot of friends. There was no one like Bay. Baylor was his person.

"I think we're going to head back to Baylor's. Your dad is getting tired."

Bandit nodded and accepted the kiss his mom placed on his cheek. "Be careful. I'll see you in the morning for breakfast."

His mom, June, swiped her lipstick from his cheek. "Okay, baby. Don't party too hard."

Bandit snorted.

June walked away, chuckling. She knew Bandit was a little too serious. He didn't really cut loose. All he did was practice and perfect his game. He didn't jump around in bounce houses or get tattooed just because there was an artist there. Bandit knew that was why Baylor had never looked at him the way he looked at Chipper. Baylor needed someone to offset his too serious nature. They were too much alike. That made for awesome friends. He supposed romantic relationships needed something more. Something he didn't have.

Bandit grabbed another glass of champagne while telling himself he could be fun. He had no idea where to start, but he could.

"Are you having a good time?"

Bandit glanced over.

Chipper waited for a response. He had really sweet brown eyes at odds with his cut body. Bandit had known him for a long time. He was glad Baylor found him.

"Yeah. I'm on like my third glass of champagne. After this, I might wander over to that adult-sized ball pit. I'm not getting in, but I'll check it out."

Chipper laughed. "Third glass? Those are rookie numbers. Take another one. One for each hand is the way to go at—whoa." At Chipper's sudden veer off topic, Bandit followed his line of sight. Baylor's assistant, Sacha, worked on keeping things running smoothly nearby. When he saw them looking his way, he immediately turned his head, as if uncomfortable with the attention.

Bandit's blood boiled. He really hated the thought of getting wiped across the floor by an MMA champ, but fuck. This was the guy's wedding, and he was already checking someone else out. Bandit tried to stay calm and keep his tone light. He chuckled. "What was that whoa all about?"

Chipper shook his head and went back to gathering glasses of champagne. "Nothing. I'm staying out of it. Forget that happened."

His blood pressure ticked higher. "No, really." This time, his tone didn't cooperate. He sounded a lot less cordial.

Chipper eyed him, as if realizing Bandit's thoughts. "Fuck. Baylor will kill me. Sacha is his friend and you're his best friend, but..." He spent a moment chewing his bottom lip. Finally, he sighed. "Please don't get me murdered on my wedding night, but when I looked up a second ago and caught Sacha looking at you, it was... intense."

Bandit glanced Sacha's way. The moment he did, Sacha looked away again. "He's not looking at me. Likely, he was just lost in thought. It happens to me all the time. I can't tell you how many times people have thought I was staring at them while my head was just somewhere else."

Chipper snorted and put a second glass of champagne in Bandit's hand. "Cool. Tell yourself that so Baylor doesn't choke me." He paused and stared at nothing for a second. "I should find Baylor. I don't hate the idea of him choking me."

Bandit shook his head as Chipper walked away. He was a mess and impossible to hate. Before Bandit could stop himself, his gaze slid Sacha's way again. Sacha turned his head. Damn. Had he really been looking at Bandit? That sounded way too good to be true, and Bandit couldn't let that thought take root in his head. He had to see Sacha all the time. Sacha ran a majority of Baylor's wedding planning company now. With quite a bit of Baylor's supplies stored at Bandit's place, they spent a ton of time in each other's company. He couldn't lie, though. Bandit would kill for a night with Sacha.

Sacha was originally from the Ukraine. He had come to America as a child but hadn't lost the thick accent. He was tall and lanky—just like Bandit. In fact, they stood eye to eye and Bandit was six three. He found that incredibly hot, especially since Sacha had the most beautiful blue eyes he had ever seen. They were always lined with dark eyeliner. He smelled good too, but Bandit knew his limits. There was no way Bandit could bag someone like Sacha. He might play pro sports and make damn good money, but Sacha was the kind of beautiful that knew its worth, while Bandit was red-haired and skinny with freckles. He had never stood out in a crowd in a good way. Not for his looks, anyhow.

The idea kept nagging at him. Bandit polished off his third and then his fourth champagne. He grabbed his fifth and decided to check out Sacha on the sly. While keeping his face turned away, his eyes slid toward Sacha. This time, he caught him staring. Whoa. Sacha might be lost in thought and not realize he was staring, but if that was his resting face, he would burn a man to the ground when they had his attention.

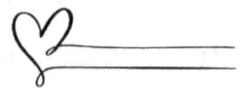

Sacha kind of wanted to slap himself. Something about watching Baylor get married was under his skin tonight. Bandit was there and Sacha couldn't stop staring every time he looked away. He was just so beautiful. On the inside too, and that shit was hot as hell. He had red hair, but his eyes were light blue. It was the rarest combination in the world. Sacha knew. He had looked it up. That summed up Bandit, though. He was a rarity. His looks bordered on boyish. He would be one of those men who looked young forever. Sacha hated how badly he craved him. He forced himself to stop looking. It was a wedding. People got frisky and went home with people they didn't know. The last thing Sacha could handle was seeing Bandit leave with someone else. He had to focus on keeping this reception moving along.

A glass of champagne appeared in front of him. "You should take a break. No one expects you to work all night."

Sacha took a breath. Bandit's usual sweet cologne washed over him. He closed his eyes and savored the smell for a second before turning. As always, those blue eyes captured him. A smile lit his face before he could stop it.

"Hey." He accepted the glass. "I know this, but Baylor means a lot to me. It's important he gets his special night." As he made the claim, Sacha's gaze moved to where Baylor stood with his sexy new husband. The child who had acted as ring bearer held Baylor's hand and spoke animatedly. Baylor hung on every word. Sacha shifted his focus back to Bandit. Bandit stared at Baylor wearing a huge grin. He had wondered more times than he should if there had ever been anything between Baylor and Bandit. Sometimes, he swore he caught Bandit looking at Baylor in just a certain way. It was probably in his head.

Bandit met his stare again, stealing his breath. "Everything is already perfect. Your job is complete."

Music began catching their attention again. As they looked on, Chipper led Baylor to the outdoor dance floor Sacha had set up. Well supervised being set up.

"The grooms' first dance, everybody."

Sacha smiled as the words came through the speakers, drowning out the music.

Bandit took back the glass he had just handed Sacha and set it on the table. "Work time is over." He grabbed Sacha's hand. "It's time to enjoy yourself." Bandit headed for the dance floor, with Sacha in tow.

Sacha tried not to obsess about the sensation of Bandit holding his hand. This wasn't a fantasy he could let grow. But then he was in Bandit's arms, and his heart did something funny. He couldn't tear his eyes away from Bandit's face. For the first time, Sacha saw the same gut-wrenching desire he felt staring back at him. But again, it was a wedding. People got weird at weddings. It was like the whole thing made people worry they would be alone forever. There was love in the air and all that. Sacha had to make this less personal.

"You look very handsome tonight." Holy shit. That was not making things less personal. He needed to keep his mouth shut. Apparently, words intended to just fall out.

Bandit's smile made Sacha forget his own name, much less any promises to himself to be quiet. "You always look stunning. I just occasionally clean up a little okay."

The claim fired something to life inside Sacha. Something fierce. It showed in his voice. "What is this cleaning up nonsense?

You are a very beautiful man. I am making lots of people jealous right now."

Bandit's huge grin never dimmed until he pulled Sacha even closer. That was the moment Sacha saw his mistake. He had been goaded into showing his hand. Bandit's expression said he knew it too. The music slowed even more and so did they. Bandit left no room between them. For a moment, Sacha thought Bandit would kiss him. At the last second, Bandit either changed his mind or always intended to keep things sweet. His lips swept Sacha's cheek. They lingered there. Sacha's heart never stood a chance against someone so much more than him. He didn't know how to explain that thought. But Sacha was just a struggling cake designer turned wedding planner. Bandit was a star. People knew his name. Not just that. People wore his name on their backs and chanted it in stands all over the world. His face was on

TVs with people cheering for him... lusting for him. It was only dumb luck Sacha had even landed in his sphere. They shared a mutual friend. That was all. Bandit would walk away from this dance and leave Sacha behind. Likely, he would never think of this again. Sacha would never think of anything else.

The songs continued, and Bandit never let him go. Even as the music moved from slow to fast and back again, Bandit kept him glued to the dance floor. Finally, the crowd wound down to only a few stragglers. Sacha had to beg out. He had more work to do. Still, Bandit held his hand as they left the dance floor, and Sacha was beyond the point of no return. Bandit was all the way beneath his skin.

"I'll stay until you're done tonight so I can walk you to your car."

Even as disappointment washed over him, Sacha knew it was for the best. He had known nothing would come of this and should be grateful for it. "There's no need. We are in a very secure location. Nothing will happen to me here."

Bandit shrugged. "I won't be able to relax until I know you're safe for the night."

That was sweet. "If you must."

Bandit's laugh eased the pressure in his chest. "I can go stand over there." He motioned toward the champagne fountain. "If my company is that bad."

Sacha rolled his eyes. "No need to be dramatic and dig for compliments. You know I like your company."

The triumph in Bandit's expression let Sacha know he had walked straight into another of Bandit's traps. "Good. How can I help?"

Sacha studied the backyard of the compound the couple had been loaned for the wedding. The ocean backdrop looked beautiful. The last few lingerers were being led away by the heavy security the owner had hired. Sacha didn't know much about him except he was someone important. A crew had arrived, and the inflatables were already deflated. A cleaning crew worked to clear away the mess. All the equipment and whatnot would be picked up by the rental company.

Sacha motioned toward the table filled with gifts. "I told Baylor I would take care of ensuring his gifts got delivered to their house so he would be free to go straight to their room. So, really, that's all I need to do."

Bandit nodded. "Cool. You grab a stack, and I will too. We'll have this knocked out in no time."

In unison, they moved to the table and grabbed boxes. "I'm thinking I'll have to make more than one trip. Luckily, their place isn't that far. When I offered to do this, I didn't consider how many gifts a celebrity would get."

Bandit chuckled. "Yeah. This is a little crazy. I can't imagine they need any of this."

"They asked people to donate to the Kapra Foundation in lieu of gifts, but it doesn't look like anyone listened."

"I did." Bandit sounded serious and so at odds with his earlier self. "The Kapra Foundation works to rescue, rehabilitate, and re-home victims of sex trafficking. They mostly work with kids. That's something that should be important to everyone, but for Baylor, that probably means everything."

Sacha nodded as he listened. "I imagine it does. Even though I don't have the same funds as the people attending tonight, I donated as well. Admittedly, I didn't really look into the foundation. I just hit the donate button. It was Baylor's wish, so..." Sacha shrugged.

Two huge guards appeared at their sides, carrying more gifts and distracting them from their conversation. Even though Sacha was grateful for their help, they cut down on the amount of time he got to spend with Bandit. The guards offered to help deliver the gifts, ensuring everything made it in one trip.

Bandit saved his mood from spiraling. "I'll help you unload all this at Baylor's. That's where I'm staying while I'm in town anyhow."

Sacha froze. He had been way too busy prepping the ceremony and reception to realize that tidbit. A nervous laugh escaped him. "Yeah. Me too."

Thankfully, Bandit immediately made things less awkward. "My parents are staying as well."

"That's nice." His parents would definitely stop Sacha from doing anything he couldn't take back.

Bandit nodded. "Chipper put them in a room in the back corner of the house, so they shouldn't even hear us banging around."

Everything inside Sacha stilled. "Banging around?"

"Putting away these gifts." Bandit's expression was so innocent. Yet Sacha got the feeling his words had been purposeful.

Sacha shifted from foot to foot at the door of his rented SUV. "Ah. Okay. Well, I will see you there, I suppose."

Bandit flashed a sweet smile. "Okay. I'll see if one of these guards will give me a ride. My parents and I rode together."

Sacha huffed before he could stop it. "You know damn well you can ride with me. Why are you acting all..." Sacha waved his hands, searching for the words. He hated it when English failed him. "I don't know the word. Get in the car."

With a laugh, Bandit jogged to the passenger side and climbed inside. Sacha's irritation didn't let up. Bandit had really acted like Sacha would just leave him there. Maybe he didn't really think of them as friends. Sacha had never considered that. Now that he had, the thought pissed him off and hurt his feelings. He was very frustrated tonight. His emotions were all over the place. He was on the road before Bandit touched his arm.

"I'm sorry. I didn't want to assume anything. It was never my intention to upset you."

Well, now Sacha felt dumb. "I am... I don't know how to say." He scrambled again. Normally, he was very good with English. He had lived here a long time, but Ukrainian was all that had been spoken in his household. When he got overly emotional, it made it hard for him to focus.

"It's okay," Bandit said, making it worse.

Sacha blew out a sigh. "It's not. I don't want you to apologize for something so unimportant."

"Your feelings aren't unimportant."

Sacha's eyes stung. He didn't need this crush to get any bigger. Thoughts of Bandit already filled too many hours. "Your feelings matter to me too." It was all Sacha could think to say. Thankfully, Chipper's house came into view. Sacha pulled into the driveway. The two guards followed. The three of them set to work.

Each time Bandit passed him, their gazes met and held. Heat built between them. Sacha couldn't pretend he didn't see his desire reflected back at him. His feelings were confirmed by the men helping them. Not on purpose, of course. They were Russian and spoke only Russian to each other. While most Russians couldn't understand Ukrainian, a few Ukrainians understood Russian. It had a lot to do with the complexities of linguistics, but for Sacha, it had more to do with where he had lived in Ukraine. He had been on the border where both languages were taught. Sacha understood every word the pair said.

They passed, eyeing Bandit and him. The bigger of the two spoke. "They should just fuck. Watching this dance is exhausting."

"They might if we hurry up and leave."

Sacha stumbled at the smaller guard's response. To his surprise and joy, no one saw. If they were this obvious, then Sacha wasn't only seeing what he wanted. He was in trouble. They would soon be alone. Baylor and Chipper stayed where the wedding was held and would leave from there to their honeymoon destination in the morning. Bandit's parents were there, but Sacha hadn't seen them. They were likely sleeping in some deep recess of Chipper's enormous house. It would be just the two of them. He should run.

"That's everything. Zander's guards are gone. I tried to tip them for their help and they laughed at me. Not sure what that was about."

Sacha's hands rose and fell. "Who knows?" He shifted from foot to foot. "I guess I should head to bed."

The disappointment Bandit tried to quickly mask made Sacha's heart soar before reality brought him back down. They couldn't do this. Bandit shifted from foot to foot. "Yeah. Me too. Goodnight."

"Goodnight."

With a final awkward glance, they headed for the hall. They laughed as they realized they were headed in the same direction. Sacha reached his room first. Bandit's was right next door. They glanced each other's way as they moved to step inside their rooms.

"Fuck it."

Before Sacha could decipher Bandit's words, Bandit was there. In his space. His mouth covered Sacha's, and the world stopped. It was nothing like he imagined. Bandit was always so gentle and sweet. His kiss was the polar opposite. Sacha's back hit the doorframe, and Bandit consumed him. He was all passion and fire. Sacha was just along for the ride. His mind was a blank slate. He would have done anything right then. Then it was over. Sacha's chest heaved like he had run a mile. A haze coated his vision. His body burned.

Bandit sweetly kissed his forehead. "Goodnight, Sacha."

Sacha couldn't speak. He couldn't move. All he could do was watch Bandit disappear inside his room. That had really just happened, and nothing would ever be the same again.

Chapter Two

Chapter Two

SACHA'S BEDROOM DOOR WAS still closed when Bandit left to take his parents to the airport. He had stopped and had breakfast with his parents before they left. On the way back to the house, he ran through a drive-thru and grabbed Sacha coffee and a breakfast sandwich. He didn't know if Sacha slept late or avoided him. Either way, Bandit didn't like it. He knew he had taken a risk, but he had to know. Now Bandit had no doubts. Sacha wanted him too. Bandit just had to find a way to completely win him.

At Chipper's, he found Sacha heading for the kitchen. He froze when he spotted Bandit. "Oh. Hey. I thought you'd left."

"I'd never leave without saying goodbye. My parents had an early flight. I drove them to the airport."

"You didn't fly home with them?"

Obviously, he hadn't, but he got what Sacha meant. "My next game is in Arizona. I didn't see the point of flying across the country just to fly back with the team. I'll meet them there. Oh." He held up his haul. "I got you breakfast."

A sweet smile touched Sacha's lips. "You're amazing."

Those words hit him so much harder than he'd expected. Sacha was just the epitome of beauty. Bandit had never had anyone who looked like Sacha choose him, much less pick him for anything other than his career.

Bandit understood his weaknesses. Being conventionally handsome was definitely not a strength he possessed. He had all the hallmarks of being teased. Red hair. Tons of freckles. Too skinny for his height.

"I hope you got something too and don't intend to watch me eat. There's only one cup."

Damn. He should have at least gotten a coffee so he didn't make Sacha uncomfortable. "I ate with my parents before I dropped them off. Sorry about that. I can leave you alone to eat."

They headed to the kitchen together.

Sacha shook his head. "You overthink things. I can see it. It's fine to sit with me."

He set the meal on the table as Sacha sat. Bandit chose a chair across from him. "I hope you like bacon, egg, and cheese. Breakfast choices are always limited."

"I'm not a picky eater. That comes from growing up poor. We ate what we were given or starved. You can learn to like anything."

Bandit nodded. "Same."

Sacha paused with the sandwich halfway to his mouth. "Really? I never realized."

Bandit shrugged. "Yeah. My mom was a teacher, and my dad worked at a factory. They barely got by. That's why they never fought to get custody of Baylor. They couldn't afford a lawyer or a court battle."

Sacha nodded along as he chewed.

Bandit forced a smile to his lips. He hated thinking about the helpless rage of not being able to save Baylor from an abusive foster family. "Thankfully, I got picked up by New England."

"I imagine that was quite a change in circumstances."

Sacha had no idea, and Bandit didn't really like talking about it. He changed the subject. "Have you created any amazing cakes lately?"

Baylor had discovered Sacha through his cake designs and subsequently hired him to help with his wedding planning business. Sacha made works of art. Bandit had only seen one design, and it had floored him. He wished Sacha could live that dream. As much as he was grateful for Sacha keeping Baylor from working himself to death, he wanted Sacha to have his biggest dream too.

Sacha set his sandwich aside and picked up his phone. He clicked around. "Here." He passed the device Bandit's way.

Bandit stared at the image Sacha had pulled up. It was a pumpkin. The carving was immaculate—like a creepy face etched into the skin. He was a bit confused. "You carve pumpkins too?"

A sexy grin spread across Sacha's face. "That's a cake."

Bandit looked at the photo again. "Shut up. It is not."

Sacha chuckled. "Keep scrolling."

He swiped to the next picture. A slice of cake had been carved from the pumpkin. "Holy shit. It really is cake. Are there more?"

"You can keep looking." Sacha went back to eating while Bandit scrolled through the images on his phone. He was blown away. Picture after picture of cakes that looked as if there was no chance they were anything but the object they appeared to be turned out to be cake. Bandit couldn't stop swiping. Then he hit an image of Sacha. He was shirtless. Lipstick coated his lips and eyeliner highlighted his eyes. He was posed artfully. Lace covered parts of his face, but it looked painted on rather than actual material. Bandit's gaze refused to budge. He took in every line and detail. Sacha's hair was slicked back, and his lips were parted, as if on a pant. He intrigued the hell out of Bandit.

Bandit turned the phone Sacha's way. "If I scroll and this is cake, I'm going to fucking die."

Sacha's eyes swam with laughter. "No. That one is actually me. My little brother is an art major. He needed a model for a portfolio he had to put together for an assignment."

"How did I not know you have a little brother?" Bandit felt guilty. He thought he always made a conscious effort to talk to Sacha when they saw each other.

Sacha shrugged. "I don't imagine we know much about each other at all. For example, I have no idea if you're an only child."

"I am. Do you only have the one sibling?"

"Yes."

"What's his name? How old is he? Share your life with me."

Sacha laughed at Bandit getting more over the top with each demand. "Artem is twenty. I don't mind telling you whatever you want, but you must share too."

"That's fair. Spend the day with me."

"Don't you have a game to get to?"

Bandit shrugged. "Not today. I can leave in the morning. What do you say? Want to explore the town with me?"

Sacha looked torn. "I've been here many times."

"But have you done anything other than work weddings?"

"No."

"Then let's see what this place has to offer."

Sacha's expression screamed he wanted to say yes, but still he hesitated. His chest expanded on a deep breath. He held Bandit's stare. "I like you a lot."

Hope surged inside Bandit. "I like you a lot too."

"You're my boss's best friend."

Damn. "I'm aware."

"I really need my job."

Without thinking, Bandit rolled his eyes. He stood and pulled Sacha to his feet. "I know you don't think I'd ever do anything to make you lose your job. Plus, we're just being tourists." Sacha still didn't look reassured.

Bandit huffed. "If you want, we can stay in and have sex instead. If I'm threatening your job, let's do it right." It was a joke. One Bandit had thrown out, hoping Sacha realized how ridiculous he was being over a simple day on the town. Except Sacha didn't immediately say no, and the way he chewed his bottom lip said he gave it a moment's consideration. Bandit had never wanted anything more.

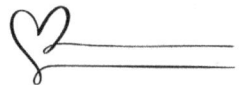

Sacha was temptation's bitch. He couldn't say yes. He wouldn't say no. How many chances would he get? Bandit was a professional athlete who could have anyone, and probably did. Sacha doubted Bandit would ever offer again. He opened his mouth to say yes. His phone rang, saving him.

Sacha turned and snatched up the device where Bandit had abandoned it on the kitchen table. Artem's name was on the screen.

Sacha quickly answered. "Hello?"

"Hey. Do you know when you're coming home? I have to work tonight, and Dana called out sick."

Sacha pinched the spot between his eyes. He couldn't ask Artem to miss work. Sacha already put too much on his shoulders. "Let me check what flights are available and see if I can move mine up. Just hold on a second." He moved the phone from his ear and opened the airline's app. With a few clicks, he found another flight. He pressed the phone to his ear again. "Okay. There's an earlier flight. Thankfully, I have TSA pre check. It's in two hours. I'll have to rush to make it."

Artem blew out a sigh of relief. "Thanks. I know I'm asking a lot, but I need a break. Forget I said that."

Sacha's chest hurt. No one understood how badly Sacha wanted Artem to be a normal twenty-year-old, having fun and enjoying his life. There were no jobs out there that paid as much as Baylor, and they couldn't afford for him to make less. Unfortunately, just existing took both of them.

"Oh, sweetheart. It's okay. I know you deserve better."

"Yeah, but now I feel bad."

"Don't." Sacha made sure Artem heard the truth in his voice. "I'll be there as quickly as I can."

"Okay. Be careful. I love you."

"Love you too, angel. Bye."

"Bye."

Sacha ended the call and focused on Bandit. The disappointment was real. He wanted this, but like Artem, he had to make sacrifices. "I have to go."

Bandit looked worried. "Is everything okay?"

Sacha nodded and headed for the hall. "My brother has to work tonight, and he's not in a position to call out."

"You have to go home for him to go to work?"

Sacha didn't look his way. "It's a long story."

Bandit followed him to the bedroom. "Do you want a lift to the airport?"

Pride made Sacha want to say no. His desire to spend every second with Bandit was stronger, and he had arranged for the rental company to pick up his SUV already, hoping to save money. "Are you sure? You've already driven there once today."

Bandit shrugged. He sat on the bed and watched Sacha gather his things. "I don't mind. If you wait on a ride, you'll never be on a plane in two hours."

That was likely true. Sacha zipped closed his suitcase.

"Plus, I'm not ready to let you go."

Sacha's gaze snapped to Bandit at the confession. He didn't know how to handle this. Unfortunately, his heart took control of his tongue. "Same."

They held each other's stare. Bandit came to his feet. Sacha's feet wouldn't budge. He watched as the space between them disappeared. Sacha swore he didn't blink as Bandit moved in and touched his lips against his. Then Sacha's eyes fell closed and the deepest longing consumed him. This was the life he craved. A life that would never be his. He had to put his family first. Artem made sacrifices. Sacha had to do the same. He could not lose his job. His family needed him. Still, Sacha didn't turn away. He was still a man in the arms of his biggest desire. Sacha would take this moment and store it away to keep like his own private treasure. Then he would steer clear of Bandit. This was the one thing that would never be.

Chapter Three

Chapter Three

THE CHEER OF THE crowd and sweat in his eyes were as familiar to Bandit as breathing. He focused on every ounce of his training, while his eyes never left the ball. His feet moved in time by muscle memory. This had been his career and life for longer than not. His parents had put him in soccer at six. He hadn't stopped since. There was nothing he didn't know about this sport. He lived and breathed for the thrill of winning.

Bandit hiked his shorts up his thighs out of habit. Sweat had the material sticking to his skin. He didn't want anything hindering his movement as he easily stole the ball from his opponent. Everything happened almost on autopilot. He practiced so much and often, this game was like breathing. Even as he quickly made his move and sent the ball sailing into the net, narrowly escaping being blocked, Bandit thought about Sacha. The crowd cheered... and booed. Someone slapped his ass. Bandit couldn't focus on any of it. No one had ever pushed their way into his mind during a match.

The rest of the game went by in a blur. They won by one. It had been a near thing, and it was because of him they almost lost. Once Sacha had shoved his way in, Bandit hadn't known how to shut out the noise. This wasn't him. It wasn't that he had never felt this way. Except maybe he hadn't ever felt like this. There was just something he couldn't shake. As Bandit stood beneath a scalding hot shower, it hit him. He knew what had him in knots. Sacha felt the same. Bandit had seen the longing in him, and that was something Bandit hadn't seen before. He had bagged his fair share of cleat chasers and ultras. He didn't think he had ever experienced true passion. Unrequited love. Now Bandit had done that. Bandit was twenty-seven. He knew he was still young, but he had watched several friends get married and grow families. Meanwhile, he focused on work and tried not to look too closely at the rest. His teammates had no trouble leaving the game, going straight to some party, and then on to a stranger's bed. Honestly, Bandit was a little awkward when it came to sex. He hated to admit it, even to himself, but damn near everyone he had ever slept with had been because they chased him and initiated things. Then he had gone along because it was sex and he didn't know how to go after the people he wanted. Sacha was different in every way. He had been braver with him than ever before. Bandit couldn't let off the gas now.

With his freedom secured for the next three days and determination in his heart, Bandit drove straight from the airport to a flower shop the moment his plane landed back home. It was nearly nine at night, and he had no idea if Sacha would even be home. The only reason he even knew where Sacha lived was because he had dropped a box of wedding shit on his porch for Baylor when Baylor had gotten sick about six or seven months back.

Flowers in hand, Bandit jogged up the front steps of the red brick townhouse. Bandit hesitated, giving himself a moment for courage. He eyed the building. It was three stories, but the front steps went to the second floor, as if the first was basement space or maybe had a garage in the back. It was squeezed between two identical townhomes. The place looked nice. He took a deep breath and held it before pushing the doorbell. Bandit tried to keep his mind blank. He couldn't let himself start overthinking. Sacha had blatantly kissed him back. He wasn't imagining things between them. The door swung open. A younger and less jaded-looking version of Sacha stared out at him. He immediately smiled.

"Oh. I can't wait to see this." He took a step back. "Come in."

Bandit was confused as fuck. He knew for a fact they hadn't met. Still, he tried to play it cool. "You must be Artem."

"I'm surprised you know that, but yeah. We watched your game earlier. Congrats on your win."

That somewhat explained Artem's reaction to him showing up at their door. Sacha had obviously at least mentioned they knew each other. "Thanks. I guess you know already, but it still feels rude not to say it. I'm Bandit."

They shook hands.

Artem's eyes flashed with humor. "Oh, I know it."

Bandit was confused as fuck. "Okay. Well." He cleared his throat. "Is—"

"Who was at the..." Sacha rounded the corner. His words died the moment their eyes met.

Artem chuckled. "Look. It's Bandit. I've told him to stay for dinner."

That absolutely hadn't happened, but Bandit smelled something delicious, and seeing Sacha made him hungry as hell.

Sacha said something in Ukrainian that made Artem chuckle, but he walked away, leaving them alone.

Bandit waited until Artem was out of sight before holding out the roses he held. "I didn't come empty-handed. For you... obviously."

A sexy smile snapped to Sacha's lips. He crossed the room and accepted the flowers. "Thank you. They're beautiful." He eyed the bouquet for a moment before meeting Bandit's stare again. "I can't believe you're here. Weren't you just in Texas?"

Bandit nodded. "That's pretty much my life. Fly in. Play a game. Fly home. I don't do a lot of staying overnight in other cities. Honestly, it's not safe. Soccer fans can be a little violent when their team loses. Plus, it's cheaper for the team to fly us back home immediately rather than also pay for overnight accommodations. Unless it's a night game, of course."

Sacha held his stare and nodded along as if Bandit was all that existed in the world. He felt seen and heard. "I'm happy to see you."

A smile exploded across his face. "Me too. I'm sorry I burst in at dinner time."

Sacha shook his head. "It's fine. We're getting a late start tonight. Are you hungry?"

"Actually, yes. I kind of rushed here from the airport, so I didn't think about food."

For a moment, Sacha simply stared at him like he didn't know what to say. Bandit shifted from foot to foot. The longer Sacha didn't speak, the more Bandit wondered if he came on too strong. He wasn't used to feeling the way he did for Sacha. Bandit equally sucked at putting himself out there like this. Finally, Sacha cleared his throat. "I'm honored I made you forget to eat."

God. He was so fucked.

Sacha turned and motioned for Bandit to follow. "Come on. We have plenty. My baba believes in cooking like she's feeding an army."

Bandit followed. He was mildly confused by Sacha's living arrangement. Since he had been asked to leave the things Sacha needed for an upcoming wedding on the porch that one time, he assumed Sacha wasn't home and lived alone. Now it seemed there were at least two other people who lived there. He had no idea what a baba was. They rounded the corner into the eat-in kitchen. Artem sat at the table along with an elderly woman and what looked to be a private nurse.

The elderly woman looked his way, and a bright smile lit her features. "Look. It's that boy Sacha is always drooling over on the TV."

The table banged.

Her gaze turned on Artem. "Why are you kicking me?"

Bandit couldn't stop smiling.

Sacha had a hand over his eyes. After a moment, his shoulders straightened, and he motioned toward the table. "You've already met Artem. This is my *babusia*. Grandmother," he explained as he motioned toward the elderly lady. Finally, he motioned toward the nurse. "And Dana."

Dana flashed a smile and went back to work watching over Sacha's grandmother.

Sacha motioned toward Bandit. "This is Bandit." He looked Bandit's way. "You can sit wherever you like. I'll find a vase for these."

With a nod, Bandit headed for the table. He wasn't one to get nervous when meeting new people. His career meant talking to strangers all the time. As he sat, Sacha's grandmother jumped right in.

"You will call me Baba. It's obvious no one feeds you. It's good you came here."

Bandit fought a laugh. He had been skinny his entire life. Each time he had gained a little weight as a kid, he had immediately had a growth spurt, seemingly stretching him several inches overnight. It drove his mom nuts.

"I appreciate the meal. It smells amazing and I'm starving after today's game." He hoped mentioning his game would drive Baba to tell him more about Sacha's drooling. He wasn't disappointed.

Baba nodded. "We watched. Sacha never misses a game. He's very proud of you."

Bandit's chest warmed. His gaze locked on Sacha as Sacha moved to claim the chair beside him. "I'm pretty proud of him too. His cake designs leave me speechless."

Sacha blushed.

Baba cackled and clapped. "I love to hear such a thing. Where do you think he learned it?"

"Culinary school," Artem muttered under his breath.

Sacha chuckled.

Baba ignored them. "We used to spend all our days cooking. Even the neighbors would come to eat. They couldn't resist the smell."

Bandit hung on every word, enjoying the glimpse into Sacha's childhood. Beneath the table, his fingers linked with Sacha's. He couldn't stop smiling. While Bandit didn't know exactly where they were headed, hope ruled everything.

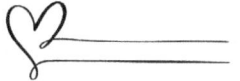

Horrified didn't begin to cover the way Sacha felt at the way Baba had embarrassed him. Ecstatic didn't begin to describe how Sacha felt at seeing Bandit. The only thing that equaled those two emotions was the terror. Sacha was scared as hell of the way Bandit made him feel. Thankfully, almost as soon as dinner was over, Artem disappeared, and Dana had put Baba to bed. It was just them.

They sat on the couch in the quiet and stared at each other. Bandit broke the silence first. "So you live with your family."

A laugh burst from Sacha. He saw the way Bandit struggled for a way to talk about the subject. No doubt it seemed odd to him.

"Yeah. That's why I said I can't do anything to jeopardize my job. My brother can't work full time to pay for college while going full time. My baba is in poor health and needs full-time nursing care while we can only afford part time. The rest is on Artem and me." Sacha blew out a sigh. Even to his ears, he sounded tired and just more tired. Unless someone had been a caregiver for a family member, they had no idea how exhausting it could be.

Bandit leaned over and snagged Sacha's waist, hauling him closer. He tucked Sacha against his side and kissed his temple. Fuck. It was just... fuck. He couldn't recall feeling warm and safe the way he did in Bandit's arms. For a moment, Bandit sat in silence with his lips pressed against his skin before speaking.

"I understand why you're worried, and I can't make you stop, but I wish you would.

You can trust me and you can trust Baylor. The way you work your ass off for Baylor outweighs my feelings. Baylor needs you so he can stay at home with Chipper and adopt all the kids. Without you, he'd have to immediately go back to working himself to death. Even if all of that wasn't the case, I'm not the kind of guy who'd run to my best friend, expecting him to fire someone because my feelings are hurt." Bandit leaned away and held Sacha's stare. He looked so sincere. "Do you honestly think that badly of me?"

Gah. He sounded so mature. There was also little doubt Bandit slept with everyone, and Sacha wasn't important enough to involve Baylor anyhow. Plus, he was so nice. "I couldn't see you hurting anyone. Off the field anyhow."

Bandit laughed.

Sacha wasn't a weakling. Under normal circumstances, he would flirt and sweep Bandit off his feet. There was nothing normal about the way Bandit made him feel. A surge of renewed confidence ran through him. Sacha shifted positions and straddled Bandit's lap, taking his power back. He wasn't a shy little bitch. He was Sacha Petrenko. Sacha didn't back down from anything. The way Bandit immediately shifted to get more comfortable and grabbed Sacha's ass to haul him closer said he, too, wasn't one to play the coward.

"We were interrupted yesterday."

Bandit didn't give him time to lower his head. He took the kiss he wanted. Sacha held on while Bandit plundered. This time, Sacha had been a little better prepared for the hungry way Bandit kissed. He still lost his breath and went hard, like going zero to a hundred.

Bandit's mouth moved from Sacha's mouth to his neck. He sucked and bit. "I have a confession. I've wanted this for a really long time."

The words snapped what little patience Sacha had left. He stood. While holding tightly to Bandit's hand, he headed for his bedroom. Sacha had wanted this for a long time too. He didn't bother turning on the lights. There was enough light filtering through the blinds from the streetlight right outside his window to find his way. Sacha didn't stop moving until they were locked inside and on the bed, picking up where they left off. He didn't want to get caught on the couch while finally getting what he always wanted.

Bandit's touch was every bit as demanding as his kiss. He had them nude in no time, but he didn't jump on Sacha. Instead, he kissed and restlessly moved against him. His skin itched with desperation to have Bandit inside him. It seemed Bandit was set on dragging things out. He thought he might scream.

"Tell me what you like?"

When Bandit's question came between kisses, it hit Sacha. He might not have been purposely torturing Sacha, but rather unsure of how to ask his preference. Sacha was too far gone.

"I want you to fuck me."

"Goddamn." The low growl nearly made Sacha blow. He was already a man on the edge. "Please tell me you have lube around here."

With a nod, Sacha rolled one way to his side table. Bandit rolled the other to find his wallet. They came together with a purpose. Bandit ripped open the condom with his teeth. Sacha made a show of lubing himself.

The moment Bandit was properly suited, his mouth covered Sacha's again. He took over the job of playing with Sacha's hole. He fingered him, stretching as he went. Sacha unabashedly rode his fingers. He was ready to fly apart.

"I feel like I'm screwing you out of some sort of foreplay or something."

Sacha grabbed Bandit's dick. "Inside me. Now." He knew how he sounded—almost inhuman in his need. It had been literally years since he'd had anything other than toys inside him. Too many times to count, those toys had filled him while he whispered Bandit's name.

Bandit didn't fail him. After hooking his arm beneath Sacha's knees, he dragged Sacha closer. His crown pressed against Sacha's asshole. He held his breath, expecting Bandit fucked the way he kissed. Bandit slowly inched his way inside. A low moan vibrated from Sacha as it happened. He thought he might fly apart.

"Damn. I swear that sound came out in your accent." Once he was fully seated, Bandit rocked, as if testing angles. "I could listen to it forever."

Another one slipped out as Bandit massaged him internally, just the way he liked.

"Yeah. Like that." That was all the warning Bandit gave before he took Sacha. Once he had Sacha moaning, begging, and tearing at his skin, Bandit never stopped pounding at the perfect angle. He kept the rhythm and speed while licking and nipping at Sacha's nipples. Sacha couldn't even think. He heard the embarrassing sounds and babbling that came from his mouth, but he had no control. Bandit was a professional athlete. He studied and practiced all the perfect moves to win. He put that same dedication into fucking Sacha.

The edge drew closer. Sacha's fingertips dug into Bandit's skin. "Oh, God. Don't stop. You feel amazing." His muscles tensed. Sacha held his breath. He focused everything on the building and tightening. Everything exploded, ripping a shout from his lungs. His body convulsed. His mouth found every place it could reach, as if praising Bandit for a job well done.

A sexy-as-hell sound came from the back of Bandit's throat. His thrusts quickened until he sawed in and out of Sacha at a rapid pace. When he blew, he whispered Sacha's name. Sacha's eyes filled with tears. He wanted to keep him.

Chapter Four

A SMILE KEPT PULLING at Sacha's lips. Their fingers played. With his head on Bandit's chest, Sacha savored the sound of Bandit's heartbeat. He couldn't sleep if his life depended on it. Happiness coated everything. He hadn't dared dream. Now he couldn't shut out the fantasies.

"How did you end up taking care of everyone?"

A sad smile pulled at Sacha's lips. He liked the way Bandit's voice vibrated against his ear while pressed against his chest, but he hadn't seen that question coming. Sacha knew he would have to answer it, eventually. It was better Bandit understood now how complicated Sacha's life was. "Do I get to ask a personal question too?"

A sexy, deep chuckle cut through the dark. Sacha's eyes closed as the sound washed over him. Hunger for a different life slammed into him. He wanted this intimacy every night forever. "You can always ask me whatever you want. I not exciting enough to have secrets."

Sacha's fingertips skimmed the sexiest of slight abs. He took a steadying breath. With his eyes closed, he could still picture the way those abs had moved and bunched. He could easily become addicted. "I disagree. I find you very exciting." The desire in his voice couldn't be missed. Sacha forced his mind away to focus on Bandit's question.

He didn't want to seem as if he avoided it. "Russia invaded Ukraine." It really was that simple and horrible.

"I'm sorry."

Sacha's hand rose and fell in a helpless gesture. He went back to stroking Bandit's stomach. "Me too. We were happy here. Sometimes it was a little crowded, being under one roof between my parents, my cousin, Artem, Baba, and me. But everyone had their own room and space. We could shut ourselves away if we needed. Then the war came, and my parents couldn't reach our family back home. My cousin, Danylo, was scared for his parents. They had sent him here because he stayed in trouble with the wrong crowd there. It truly was best for him. He ended up being a model student here. But once he couldn't reach his parents, he was determined to go home. So my parents took him. It was every bit as bad as they feared. Our family—like we once had—lived on the border and was the first to be taken." Sacha's hand fell still. Bandit covered it, as if lending him strength for—no doubt—knowing exactly how this story ended. "They were all dead. My father and Danylo were determined to stay to fight. My mother refused to leave them." Sacha shrugged. He felt the dismissive gesture happen against his will. There was no stopping the desire to minimize the pain. "They're all gone now."

"Oh my god, Sacha. I'm so sorry. Now I wish I hadn't asked. I didn't mean to make you relive all that."

He was sweet. That was what Sacha couldn't resist about him. He would never leave Sacha to run a family while barely out of culinary school. Bandit would never ask him to give up his dreams in a fight for a country that was no longer his. Sacha knew it wasn't fair to be bitter, but he was. Artem and he had given up their lives, and *that* wasn't fair. Sacha couldn't keep thinking about it. He pushed the hurt and anger from his mind to focus on Bandit.

"My turn. Have you and Baylor ever been more than friends? I've never seen two people closer." Sacha kept his tone upbeat. He didn't want Bandit to think he was jealous. Maybe a small part of him was, but not because they were friends. It was because he didn't have anyone special the way they had each other. He felt Bandit shrug.

"Not really."

His answer had a laugh bursting from Sacha. "Not really isn't a no. It's barely an answer. And after I poured my heart out," he added, being ridiculous and hoping to lighten the mood.

Bandit chuckled as he linked his fingers through Sacha's. "I mean, the two of us are closer than most, I guess. He used to sneak out or run away and stay at my house most of the time. His foster parents let it go on most nights since they got money from the state, whether he was there or not. We were typical friends growing up. He slept in my bed every night. My parents never questioned it. We were best friends. We did everything together. I've always been athletic, straight-presenting, I guess. They had no reason to think we shouldn't spend every second together. Meanwhile, I held him all night while he slept or fell apart. It was like second nature." Bandit paused for a second, as if unsure if he should continue. When he did, his tone never changed. He sounded like he talked about any memory. Like it wasn't special. Just neutral. "There were nights when that comfort turned into more, but I think it was still just a soothing

thing." He sighed, sounding exasperated. "Truthfully, this is one reason I never really talk about our friendship. It's hard to explain. He's my other half. I truly believe that, but we are genuinely only friends. We probably could've gotten married right out of high school and lived peacefully together until we died, never regretting that decision. But I was content with only having my best friend with me all the time because I was so focused on my career. Then Baylor met Freddie."

A pain sliced through Sacha at the name. Sacha had worked for Baylor since six months after he married Freddie. The pair had been amazing together and had the most beautiful child. Then they had died, and Sacha had been there to see that tiny casket and witness Baylor rage at the universe. It was something he could never unsee, and it was one of those horrible things that burned into the soul.

Bandit toyed with his fingers and kept talking. "He's still the closest person to me, but I know our friendship is just that and he would've missed out on a lot if he had settled for peace."

Sacha wondered if Bandit realized how much love was in his voice. He couldn't stop pushing. "You know, everything you've said sounds a lot like love."

"It is." Bandit didn't try to lie. Thankfully, he didn't leave things there and rip out Sacha's heart. "I love him more than anyone. It'll probably always be that way, but it's not the kind of love that I can really explain. We're friends but almost also like family, but not family because that makes things weird." He laughed. "I don't know what I'm trying to say. He knows me better than anyone. That makes him important to me, but it's not a passionate relationship. We've never seen each other that way. Not really."

Oddly, it made sense. Sometimes people needed to forget reality to survive life. There had been times when Baylor and Bandit had given each other that, but it had only been an extension of their friendship. They weren't in love. They just loved each other. There was a subtle yet huge difference.

"Have you ever had a Freddie or Chipper in your life?"

A bark of laughter made Sacha smile. "That's two questions, but no. I'm just me."

Sacha went up on one elbow. He had to see Bandit's face. "What is this only me? What does that mean?"

Bandit tucked a strand of hair behind Sacha's ear. He lingered, stroking its shell. "I'm not sure anyone looks at me like that.

Like I said, I'm not exciting, I guess. There's nothing about me that sets anyone's soul on fire. No one is dying to see me so they can simply breathe the same air. There's no one staring at me like they want to crawl beneath my skin and live there. I think I just wasn't born with whatever that trait is that makes people desirable."

For a moment, Sacha couldn't decide if he was angry or sad. He didn't understand how one person could be so blind. Either way, Sacha couldn't let Bandit continue to believe that lie. "All that is complete nonsense. I want to see you just so I can breathe the same air. There's definitely been way too many times I've stared at you and wished I could crawl beneath your skin. Or at the very least, have you notice me at all." He lowered his voice, losing his courage, but he couldn't stop. "My soul is very much on fire. You just scare the hell out of me. I don't think I have much to offer, but I have everything to lose. Tell me what I'm supposed to do with that."

Bandit took a shaky-sounding breath. "Keep seeing me. Give me a chance to take away the fear. For fuck's sake, don't tell me that shit and then walk away. How am I supposed to live with knowing I found what I want most and can't hang on to it?"

Bandit was right. It was cruel. There was something between them, and it wasn't just sex. Sacha didn't truly believe they could make it, but he wasn't ready to give up just yet. "I'm not walking away." He just hoped he didn't end up running.

Bandit rolled.

Sacha found himself beneath a hard man and all his fears scattered.

Bandit's lips skimmed his. "Good, because my soul is definitely burning and I'm about to be beneath your skin."

Goddamn. Bandit had no idea. He was already so deeply embedded in Sacha that Sacha would never shake him. That had never been the problem. The problem was how much this would hurt when Sacha's responsibilities ruined them, and they would. Life never let him keep anything. He already knew this would be no different.

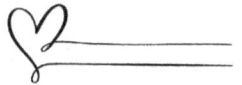

They had made love for hours. Bandit was sore, like he had spent the entire day at the gym. He knew he should go to sleep, but he couldn't stop staring at Sacha. The soft way he breathed while he slept kept Bandit fascinated. He was beyond moved Sacha had decided to put his trust in him. Bandit would never jeopardize Sacha's career. It didn't matter how much his heart ended up shit-stomped. Sacha had the kind of responsibilities no one should have at their age. Plus, Bandit just wasn't that guy. He didn't like the way it felt to hurt people, and he had to live with himself.

A loud thump and a cry had Sacha shooting from the bed—like programmed to respond. He threw on a pair of shorts that waited on a reading chair by the door and was out so fast, Bandit's mind didn't have time to catch up. He rummaged for his jeans when crying reached his ears. Bandit pulled on the pants while following the sound. His footsteps slowed as the kitchen came into view. Artem and Bandit were both half-dressed and helping Baba off the floor.

She cried and swiped at her face. "I just wanted some water."

"Did Dana not leave a glass next to your bed?"

Baba shook and looked beyond upset after her obvious fall. The brothers checked her over as if making sure she hadn't broken any bones. Even though he didn't think his presence would be welcome at such a difficult moment, he couldn't do nothing.

Sacha eyed him wearing a closed expression as Bandit stepped around them and started opening cabinets until he found the glassware. "I'll get your water if you want to head back to bed."

Baba sniffled. She didn't look his way as she said something in Ukrainian.

Artem barked out a laugh.

Sacha avoided his gaze, but his face was red. "Um. Yeah. She'd love that water. There's a filter pitcher full of water in the refrigerator."

Bandit gave a sharp nod, even though no one looked at him. "On it." He filled the glass as Sacha helped Baba from the chair they had put her in after lifting her from the floor. She leaned heavily on Sacha as they headed down the hall.

Artem reached for the glass he held. "I'll take that to her."

Bandit passed it along. "Thanks."

Artem dipped his chin and turned away. He froze and turned back Bandit's way. "Thank you. Sacha deserves to have something in his life beyond all this. He does too much for us."

Bandit heard the guilt. His heart went out to him. "You don't have to thank me for that."

A bright smile lit Artem's face. "By the way, Baba says you're a good boy, and judging by the noises you had Sacha making, you also know how to do that good fucking. Roughly translated."

A bark of laughter burst from Bandit even as horror washed over him. He hadn't considered the noise. His face had to be as red as his hair. Thankfully, Artem was already heading down the hall.

Bandit made his way back to Sacha's room. Waves of embarrassment kept washing over him. He couldn't believe Sacha's grandmother had heard all of that. Bandit didn't know how he would look her in the eye. He supposed he would find out because he wasn't going anywhere.

Bandit stripped and crawled back into bed. This final burst of adrenaline had him wiped out, and the exhaustion made itself known. He dozed without meaning to. Bandit didn't realize it until the bed dipped beside him. He reached out and hauled Sacha into his arms.

"You need some sleep, angel."

Sacha kissed his chest but didn't speak. He felt the way he shook. Bandit held him tighter and kissed his head. Sacha had tried to spare him from this. Bandit didn't want that. He had been that guy his whole life. He had taken care of Baylor, and now Sacha needed him. Bandit was more than not going anywhere now that Sacha had let him in. He was ready to take over his life.

Chapter Five

Chapter Five

SACHA THOUGHT OF NOTHING except Bandit fixing that glass of water. For most people, it was likely such a small thing. For Sacha, it was everything. No one had stepped in and volunteered a single damn thing since Baba's care had fallen on him. A simple glass of water said everything about Bandit. Sacha smiled just thinking his name.

Each time his roses died, Bandit replaced them. Currently, they were dead since they hadn't seen each other in two weeks. That was on Sacha. His schedule had been super crazy with Baylor out of town. Coupling that with Bandit's schedule made everything harder. Sacha was willing to work at it. He was still worried about Baylor's reaction, though. If Baylor flipped, Bandit would definitely choose Baylor. Bandit had assured him his job wasn't on the line. Sacha swung back and forth on if he believed that.

Sacha raced around, gathering his things. Baylor still had two days left of his month-long honeymoon. Even though he had hired two more people to help Sacha, the meetings with clients always fell to him when Baylor wasn't around. He barely had any time left before he would need to leave if he wanted to get there on time. The doorbell rang. A growl rose in Sacha's throat. He felt like his life was always like this. There was always something that needed to be done. He never got to stop and enjoy the things he actually liked doing. Sacha understood that was life. Still, sometimes, he felt like his best years were slipping away.

He rushed to the front door. As he yanked it open, his irritation died. A smile exploded across his face that came from his soul.

"Hey."

Sacha pushed aside the gorgeous roses Bandit held and captured his lips. He felt the stress fall away as their tongues played. Their kiss was a healing balm on his frayed nerves. He pulled away. "Hey." Sacha sounded breathless and didn't care.

Bandit's gorgeous smile nearly made him sigh. "Sorry for not calling first, but that was totally worth the risk."

Sacha chuckled as he stepped back, inviting Bandit inside. "I'm over the stars to see you, or whatever the saying is. Unfortunately, I also am about to leave. With Baylor still gone, I'm handling all the client meetings."

"It's okay. Five minutes is better than nothing. I could drive you."

"That's—" Sacha's phone rang, cutting off his words. He pulled it from his pocket and checked the face. "Sorry. It's Artem. Give me just a second." He put the phone to his ear. "Hello?"

"You're going to hate me."

Sacha automatically pinched the spot between his eyes. "That's not possible."

Artem blew out a tired-sounding breath, proving how overwhelmed he was too. "I know Baba has an appointment, but I won't be home in time to take her. They've moved up my project presentation to today."

Sacha found the first flat surface and sat. "What am I supposed to do? I can't take her. Baylor is still out of town and I'm meeting with a client. If I lose this big of a contract, I could lose my job. Then what? You won't have a school to do projects for. I also can't cancel Baba's appointment. She's already been waiting six months to see this specialist, and we can't afford Dana for more days this week."

"Put her in an Uber. I should be able to pick her up from the appointment."

Sacha fought the urge to growl. "Put her." He stopped and took a breath when his voice came out enraged. Sacha tempered his tone and tried again. "I can't put her in an Uber. She can't make it to the kitchen to get water without falling."

"I'll take her."

Sacha's gaze shot to Bandit. He looked completely serious. Damn. He was amazing. "I can't ask that of you."

"Is that Bandit?"

Sacha ignored Artem's question. "Baba is a handful. She can barely walk any longer and... well, you've met her."

Bandit chuckled. He was so goddamn sexy. "I know all of that. It's fine. If she'll let me, I'll take her. Then we can spend time together after your appointment."

Something grew inside Sacha as he stared at Bandit.

"Sorry, Sacha. I have to go. Love you." Artem disconnected the call before Sacha had time to respond.

Sacha clutched the phone between his hands. Hope and guilt built inside him. "I just..."

Bandit set the flowers on the coffee table next to Sacha and pulled him to his feet. He kissed Sacha's forehead. "It's okay, gorgeous. You're not alone. I know if I needed you, you'd have my back. It's part of being in a relationship. We're a team."

Sacha's throat swelled. "We're in a relationship?"

Bandit looked confused. "Was that not understood?"

Sacha shot forward and stole another kiss. "I'm lucky as hell to have you. I swear I'll make this up to you." Sacha had no clue how. It would probably be sexual. He couldn't wait.

Bandit kissed his cheek and then swiped another sweet kiss across his lips. "Just give me all the information I need and go to your meeting. I've got Baba." His lips swept Sacha's mouth, as if sweetly calming him. "I've got you."

Sacha didn't deserve him. He honestly didn't know how he had landed this out-of-this-world man, but Sacha planned to do everything he could to keep him. Bandit already had him addicted.

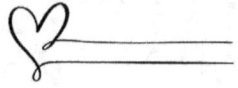

There had been a small part of Bandit that expected to regret volunteering. Universally, no good deed went unpunished. His day with Baba had been nice. Bandit's grandparents were either not in his life or had already passed. All he had were his parents. Even when his grandmother had been alive, she never really had much to do with him. She had been a hands-off grandparent. She believed she had done her job, raising her kids, and now she was done. He understood, but he realized now how much he had missed. Bandit might have been the one doing all the work, but she wouldn't stop trying to spoil him. They stopped for ice cream before heading home. Baba was visibly ready for bed by the time they came through the door.

Sacha met them as they stepped inside. "Hey. How did the doctor's appointment go?"

"I'm old."

Sacha rolled his eyes at Baba's response. "Did you learn anything?"

"That I'm old."

Sacha huffed.

Baba patted Bandit's hand. "Thank you for going with me today. It was fun. Kiss me and I'll head to bed."

Bandit didn't point out it was still late afternoon. He kissed Baba's cheek. "Thank you for spending time with me."

She chuckled and let Sacha help her to her bedroom.

Bandit wandered toward the kitchen. He caught sight of the fresh flowers in a vase on the counter. Sacha deserved nice things. He wished Sacha would let him do more than bring him flowers. While he knew they hadn't been officially dating that long, they had known each other and been in each other's lives for years. Bandit wanted to do more.

Sacha molded against his back and kissed his nape. "Mhmm. This spot is sexy." His lips skimmed the back of Bandit's neck again. "Thank you so much for helping me today. You have no idea how much it means to me."

Bandit turned and wrapped his arms around Sacha, blatantly touching his ass. "It was fun. I've never really had much of a grandmother experience. Thank you for letting me borrow yours."

Sacha's smile was everything.

Giving in to temptation, Bandit touched his lips to Sacha's cheek and kissed a path to his ear. "Plus, I wore her out and now we get to play."

The sound of Sacha's soft laughter warmed his chest. "Absolutely. You definitely deserve a treat after that."

Bandit started to ask what Sacha wanted to do for the rest of the night, blowing off trading favors as a joke. After all, he hadn't helped Sacha for any reason other than he cared. He didn't want Sacha thinking he was only there for one thing. Before he said a word, Sacha took his hand and headed for the bedroom. Bandit wouldn't say no.

The moment they were shut inside, Sacha headed for the bed. He sat on the edge and pulled Bandit forward to stand between his knees. Bandit couldn't blink against the sight of Sacha's lust. He genuinely looked hungry for Bandit. Something surged through him he couldn't name. Then Sacha kissed his stomach. Bandit's body fired to life. But he still couldn't do anything except stare down at Sacha as Sacha unzipped Bandit's pants.

As Sacha set his erection free, Bandit couldn't do it. He couldn't let Sacha believe he was there for any reason other than he wanted to be. He cupped Sacha's chin and tilted it upward, forcing Sacha to meet his stare. The open yearning in Sacha's expression nearly buckled his knees.

"I'm sorry. I have to have you."

Bandit pushed, sending Sacha tumbling onto his back as Bandit went to work on his clothes. In between stripping Sacha, he tore his way out of his clothes. Once they were both nude, Bandit fell on him like a starving man. The way they came at each other was like they wanted to be beneath each other's skin. Bandit had never felt this way. They barely had a condom in place and a mess of hastily spread lube before Bandit was inside Sacha. With their palms flattened against each other and their fingers linked, they strained toward the same goal. Sweat coated his body. Their kiss was every bit as violent as the sex. The way Sacha made him feel like there was no other man desired more than him was addictive. He was scared no one else would ever be enough again. Bandit also hoped he wouldn't have to find out. As he watched Sacha come unglued while poised on the edge, he prayed this was forever. This was the one he wanted.

Chapter Six

Chapter Six

WATCHING BANDIT SCORE NEVER got old. His pride and excitement could practically be felt through the TV. Bandit had offered him tickets since it was a hometown game, but Sacha had to stay with Baba, and actually going to a game was too much for her. Baba talked nonstop about Bandit when he wasn't around. Bandit had jumped into their family and became one of them like he had always been meant for Sacha. It was nice. Baba adored him.

He supposed Baylor knew they were a couple by now. They never talked about it, and Baylor stayed wrapped up in his new marriage. Honestly, it was the best scenario as far as Sacha was concerned. He didn't want a big discussion over the matter. Sacha just wanted happiness.

Bandit scored.

Baba moved closer to the TV, nearly an inch from the screen.

Sacha huffed but didn't bother complaining.

Baba poked the screen. "I don't like that one. That one keeps touching our man."

Sacha swiped his hand over his mouth, hiding a smile over Baba calling Bandit their man. He tried reassuring her. "They're teammates and they're winning. It's common to slap each other's asses and whatnot."

With a shake of her head, Baba reclaimed the chair she had pulled close to the TV. "No. That one takes advantage. His hands are always stealing gropes. Any excuse, no matter how small. Trust your baba. That one is no good."

Sacha shook his head and went back to watching the game. Unfortunately, the seed had been planted. Sacha couldn't stop watching the dark blond with wandering hands. Baba was right. It was odd. He slapped Bandit's ass over every small thing. Big things had the guy hugging him from behind. His actions more than bordered on inappropriate. They were downright pissing Sacha off. He read the guy's number and searched online to get a name. Tip Ramos. He was nearly thirty. One of the oldest members on the team. To Sacha's disgust, he was handsome. His net worth put Sacha to shame, making him look exactly like the pauper he was. Sacha felt sick. He had always known he couldn't compete. Seeing Bandit's options firsthand was different. His chest hurt. The game was definitely ruined. Even when they won, Sacha couldn't bring himself to cheer. Artem came through the door and Sacha immediately headed for his bedroom. He wanted to feel bad about not letting Artem as much as sit down before shifting responsibility to his shoulders, but Sacha felt heartsick. Things had been so intense with Bandit. Sacha hadn't even considered Bandit might cheat. That seemed crazy now that he thought about it. Bandit had all the opportunities in the world, while Sacha simply added Bandit to his daily juggling act. Why would Bandit stay faithful?

Sacha rubbed his temples and paced the floor. They hadn't made plans for tonight since Artem hadn't known what time he would be home. Sacha wanted to text Bandit and beg him to come straight there, but he was a little scared of himself. There was no way he could hide the growing desperation inside him. He had been so certain they were headed places, but now he saw every crack. They had been dating for four months and Bandit hadn't said he loved Sacha or talked about their future. Maybe that was normal, but they felt hotter than anything Sacha had ever experienced. He thought they both felt it—like they had each met the one. Now he felt dumb. They hadn't actually set boundaries for their relationship. Maybe Sacha didn't even have a right to be angry. Could he expect Bandit to be faithful when he had never said he expected as much? Everything felt like a nightmare. They had to talk. Sacha found his phone. He doubted Bandit was anywhere near able to text him back yet, but Sacha had to try.

Sacha: *Yay! Congratulations on your win. How do you plan to celebrate?*

There. He didn't sound crazy. Sacha simply sounded like a boyfriend, gently inquiring what Bandit would do next. He paced and chewed the side of his nail. Sacha didn't want to beg Bandit to come over. He needed Bandit to choose him. The phone buzzed, nearly sending his heart flying out of his chest. He scrambled to open the text.

Bandit: *Hey baby. Thank you. I'm headed to Area 9 to get drinks with Tip.*

Fuck! Area 9 was a club downtown that catered to the upper class. Sacha had set up weddings there. That was the only time he ever stepped foot in the building. He didn't fit there. Still, Sacha tried not to slip into insanity. That was unattractive and so much was already stacked against him.

Sacha: *Okay. Have fun. Miss you.*

Bandit: *Will do. Miss you too.*

Okay. Sacha told himself that was enough. Bandit missed him. Surely he wouldn't have said as much if he didn't mean it. Except Sacha had said it first and cornered him. Goddamn it. He couldn't do it.

Sacha: *You know that Tip guy has a thing for you, right?*

As soon as Sacha hit send, he regretted it. Why had he done that? This was a bad look.

Bandit: *No, he doesn't. We're just teammates and friends. The two of us have been on the same team longer than any other players. That's it. He just needs me tonight.*

In other words, Bandit fully intended to go on a date with another man, even after having the truth pointed out to him. Sacha fought a growl. Bandit had always been a blind one.

Sacha: *He touches you too much. I don't like it.*

Bandit: *Baby, I can't tell a teammate not to touch me.*

He was right. Sacha tossed his phone on the bed. His chest hurt. He had lost. If Sacha pointed out the obvious and Bandit still argued, that only proved this was a purposeful act. He chose Tip because that was exactly where he wanted to be. Sacha didn't know why he had been so blind, but he was tired. Life had just fucking beat him. He never got to do anything fun while also watching Bandit choose someone else. Everything was responsibility and the weight of everything crushed the breath from his chest. He headed for the kitchen. Dana helped Baba cook. Artem did his homework at the table. Sacha opened the freezer, grabbed a full bottle of vodka, and headed back to his bedroom without looking anyone's way. He would lock himself in his bedroom and give himself one night to mourn. Tonight, he couldn't handle anything else.

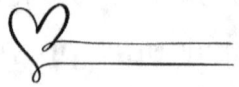

Bandit texted several times and called enough to make himself look crazy. Sacha wouldn't acknowledge him. He wasn't good at relationship type stuff and Sacha had never shown a hint of jealousy before. Bandit was at a loss. Music thumped around him. Tip stayed glued to his side. At first, Bandit chalked it up to them being there together, but Sacha's claims ate at him.

"Do you want to dance?"

Bandit glanced Tip's way at the offer. He didn't look like a guy coming onto him. Bandit didn't know what to think. "No thanks. I'm a little tired tonight. Hey, I'm going to step outside for a second. I need to make a call."

Tip nodded. If he was disappointed, he didn't show it. As Bandit stepped outside, he swallowed his pride and texted Artem.

Bandit: *Do you have any clue what's up with Sacha? I'm getting worried. He won't answer the phone.*

Artem: *Don't know. I've been busy with homework. He stormed through here a couple of hours ago, grabbed some vodka, and locked himself in his room. I figured it was work related. His job can be pretty taxing.*

Fuck his life. It was that bad. He didn't know what to do. Like he had said, he couldn't tell a teammate not to touch him. Not only was that humiliating, it was ridiculous. That was part of the game. Part of his job. Nothing had changed in four months. He didn't understand why it was a problem now.

"Everything good?"

Bandit startled as Tip appeared at his side. "Yeah. I just had to check on something." He needed someone to talk to, but it couldn't be the guy who was the problem. That seemed counterintuitive.

Tip smiled. "Cool. Since you're not in the mood to dance, you should come back to my place."

Goddamn it. Sacha had him questioning everything. Not once had he bailed on his teammates if they needed him. When Tip had invited him out, he had seemed off. Sacha hadn't felt like he could abandon him.

"Um." Bandit didn't know what to do. "I kind of have to take care of something, and—like I said—I'm pretty exhausted."

Tip's smile grew. He was closer, and Bandit didn't think he had seen him move. "That's okay. I can take you to do whatever. Then I could do all the work."

Bandit's mind stuttered to a stop. He didn't want to misunderstand. "What work?"

Tip laughed. He shuffled even closer. "Come on, Bandit. You know I'm retiring after this year. Pretty soon, we won't have anything holding us back. We can stop toeing the line."

Bandit's mind raced in so many directions, he couldn't catch a thought. Had they been toeing the line? What had he been doing that looked that way? What the fuck was happening?

Before Bandit saw it coming, Tip swept in for a kiss. Only the shock held him still for long enough for Tip's lips to land. He immediately took a step back. "Damn, man. I'm seeing someone."

Tip's hazel eyes showed his hurt before he straightened away. "I thought..."

Goddamn it. Sacha had been right about everything. Still, he had games left to play with Tip. He had to smooth things over. "I'm sorry for whatever I did to give you the wrong impression. I've got a good thing going and I don't want to ruin it."

"You never bring anyone around. There's nobody at our games."

That was hard to explain. "He works a lot." Okay. Maybe it wasn't that hard.

A deep line appeared between Tip's eyebrows. "Why? He has you. This is starting to feel like a made-up guy."

Well, it was official. Bandit had failed on every level with Sacha. Even Tip knew it, and he thought Sacha was imaginary. Bandit rubbed his forehead.

For lack of any idea of what to do, Bandit woke his phone and showed Tip his wallpaper. It was a picture of Sacha and him together.

Tip eyed the phone. He blew out a low whistle. "Okay. I see your point." His gaze shifted to Bandit. "Still, I have to say, for someone who doesn't want to fuck up anything, you've been throwing off a lot of strong signals and you didn't hesitate to accept this date."

Bandit pinched the spot between his eyes. "I didn't know it was a date." He dropped his hand. Bandit didn't want to deal with this. He wanted to find Sacha and plead his case.

Tip took a step back. He looked uncomfortable. "All right. My bad."

"Let's forget this happened."

Tip nodded. "Okay." It didn't sound okay. Tip walked away, proving his thoughts correct.

Bandit turned his chin up and stared at the sky. He thought he always tried so hard, but being the good guy had bitten him in the ass. On top of that, it looked as if he should've been offering some sort of financial support to Sacha. He hadn't thought Sacha would ever allow that. His pride would never. From the outside looking in, it just seemed like he let Sacha down on every level. He didn't bring him to the games. He didn't help alleviate his burden. It seemed he also went on dates with other men. Goddamn it. He tried again to call. Bandit was determined to admit Sacha had been right and throw himself on his mercy. As his call went unanswered, Bandit had to admit the truth. He had destroyed the best thing to ever happen to him and he hadn't even known he was doing it.

Chapter Seven

Sacha dragged himself from bed, feeling thirty years older. His head hurt. It felt like the desert lived in his mouth and his eyes were on fire. Somehow, he made it through a shower, but he didn't bother trying to look pretty. As he stepped from his bedroom, he spotted the flowers. They were everywhere. Sacha turned in a circle. Baba sat on the couch with Dana, smiling.

"They haven't stopped coming all morning."

Sacha didn't know how to react. He didn't want to tell Baba about Bandit's cheating and break her heart, but neither could he find an ounce of forgiveness.

"You don't look happy. Are these the gift of a guilty conscience?"

Sacha worked up a smile he didn't feel. "No. I'm just overwhelmed and not feeling great."

Baba nodded. "Okay. I'd hate to curse the boy. It's been a long time since I dragged out my magic, but I would for you."

Sacha's smile turned genuine. "I know, Baba." The doorbell rang, saving Sacha from their conversation. If it was more flowers, he would tell them to take them back and not darken his door again. Bandit didn't mean it. Flowers were a cheater's gift. They made Sacha's chest hurt. Baylor and Chipper stood on the steps, waiting. Sacha suddenly wished he had bothered a little with his appearance.

"Hey. This is a nice surprise." He hoped. Damn. It was possible this had to do with Bandit and he might be fucked.

Baylor flashed a bright smile. "Hi, gorgeous. It's so good to see your face."

Sacha waved them inside. "I know. It feels like we're always missing each other."

Baylor nodded as he stepped inside. "To be fair, I barely work anymore." He paused halfway to the kitchen. "Holy shit, Sacha. Is there a reason you have a flower shop in your house?"

Sacha waved away the question and rushed the pair to the table before Baba butted in. "It's a project."

"Oh." Baylor blinked. Chipper pulled a chair out for him. "I'll admit I haven't kept up with things the way I should."

Sacha waited until Chipper sat before joining them. "It's okay. You're still newlyweds. You're allowed to bask."

Chipper winked.

Everything inside Sacha sighed. Some people really got it all.

Baylor shifted nervously, setting alarm bells clanging in Sacha's head. "Actually, that's kind of why I'm here. When Chipper and I got married, we already knew we wanted to adopt. With Zander's help, it'll probably happen very quickly and we'll be dealing with what'll likely be a special needs child."

Fuck. He was about to be given even more work. His chest felt like it might cave.

"So, I've made one of the hardest decisions of my life to dissolve my business."

It was worse. He couldn't breathe, but Baylor kept talking like he hadn't ripped the rug out from beneath Sacha.

"I don't want to split my time and travel with a child who'll likely have a lot of separation issues already. It wouldn't be fair. Plus, after losing Micah, I don't know if I can handle being away from another child."

Everything he said was fair, but not to Sacha. He tried not to hyperventilate.

"But I also don't want you to think I'd just leave you like this, so Chipper and I have a proposal for you. We'd like to fund a startup. You're the most talented cake artist I've ever seen in my life, and in my business, I've seen a lot. We already have thirty orders lined up for you at two thousand a cake."

Sacha blinked. He couldn't breathe for a new reason.

Baylor didn't seem to notice. "Don't worry. You know I'm good at scheduling. There's no time crunch. I calculated plenty of time for each creation. I also left plenty of space for you to take on more orders. So, what do you say?"

Sacha was stunned speechless. "I don't know what to say. There are so many details. How much percentage will I get of these orders?" Sacha hated to be all about the money, but he kind of had to be.

Baylor made a dismissive motion. "I won't be taking a percentage. Plus, I've already deposited a severance check of seven hundred and fifty thousand into your account. That's five years' pay. Hopefully, that'll be enough to get you started."

Artem burst through the door and threw his backpack away as he ran toward Sacha. He skidded to a stop and didn't bother saying hello before shoving his phone beneath Sacha's nose. Sacha's chin dropped. His hands shook as he reached for the device. He felt the final pieces of his heart shatter. There it was. Tip kissing Bandit. He supposed it was some sort of gossip article, but the proof was still the same.

Sacha passed the phone back to Artem. "I'm sorry. Please excuse me." That was all he managed before he darted for his bedroom. He couldn't deal with anything else today.

Sacha sat on the edge of the bed and wrapped his arms around his stomach. He felt like he would fly apart if he took too deep of a breath. A light knock sounded before Baylor walked in without waiting for an invitation. He sat next to Sacha and squeezed him against his side. Sacha lost the battle. Tears flowed down his cheeks as silent sobs racked his body. He had known, but seeing it was more than he could take. Sacha had honestly thought it was love. He was so fucking ridiculous. Of course, Bandit wouldn't love someone like him.

Baylor kissed his temple. "Let it out. Do you want to break something? I could drive you to go slash his tires."

Despite everything, a watery laugh escaped Sacha. "I'm sorry. You shouldn't be in the middle. I know he's your best friend."

"You're my friend too, and I love you. There's nothing, not even this, that you can't bring to me. I'm sorry I introduced you two. Not once did I think Bandit would do something like this."

Sacha let Baylor hold him. "Me either, but here we are." He straightened. Sacha had too many people depending on him to fall apart. "Thank you for helping me get started on something new. I pray I don't fail you." Or his family.

Baylor rubbed his back. "Don't worry. Chipper knows literally everyone on the planet. He'll keep orders headed your way. We never would've made this decision at your expense. But it's okay to focus on yourself for a bit. You've existed for everyone else for years. Take a minute to breathe. I promise money isn't something you'll have to worry about."

Baylor was right. Chipper knew everyone. He would probably be swamped with orders. Sacha should be thrilled. He never thought he would get to live his dream. But this was his life and that meant he wouldn't get to enjoy a single moment of happiness over it. He didn't know where to go from here.

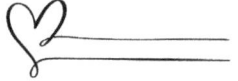

Bandit's chest hurt every second of the day. He had wanted to show up on Sacha's front porch first thing this morning, but he had mandatory team practice. This wasn't a job from which he could call out sick. Bandit was contractually obligated to be here. Thankfully, it was over, and he was five minutes away from being out the door.

While bent and tying his shoes, a silence fell over the locker room. It was followed closely by some rumblings about it being a long time and condolences. Before Bandit could figure out what happened, a very enraged-looking Baylor hovered over him.

"Never in our entire lives have I been so goddamn mad at you. What in the hell were you thinking? If you didn't want Sacha any longer, you should've broken things off before landing online kissing someone else."

Oh, fuck. Surely not. "What?"

"Don't play dumb." Bandit had never seen Baylor like this, and he had seen a lot of sides of Baylor.

"I'm not trying to. I just genuinely don't know what in the hell you're talking about."

"Um." Tip shuffled closer and flashed his phone Bandit's way. There it was. A picture of Tip kissing him. His gaze shot to Tip. Tip looked as shocked as him. He wouldn't want this either. This was their career. More than anything, this definitely destroyed his relationship.

Bandit stood and grabbed his bag. "It's not what it looks like. I have to get to Sacha."

"Not what it looks—what? Surely that's not the bullshit you're about to feed Sacha. You've decided to fucking gaslight him?"

All eyes were on them. Bandit wondered if he would faint. His world was crashing down on him, and he couldn't breathe.

"It genuinely isn't how it looks," Tip cut in, bringing Baylor's wrathful look his way. Tip held up his hands in surrender. "Seriously. Go with Bandit and let him explain."

Bandit took Baylor's arm and steered him from the room. He didn't meet anyone's stare or say a word until they were outside. He saw Chipper waiting, but he didn't approach. That was good. Bandit was on his last string.

He spun and focused on Baylor. "I didn't cheat. Let's get that out of the way."

Baylor gave him a sharp nod, proving he would listen.

Bandit took a breath. Baylor believed. That mattered as much as Sacha believing. "Last night, I just thought a teammate was asking me to drinks to celebrate. It never occurred to me it might be more. Sacha tried to tell me Tip had a thing for me, but I wouldn't listen because I'm just me. Why would anyone have a thing for me?"

"Because you're gorgeous and nice," Baylor said, cutting in.

Bandit ignored him and kept talking. "Anyhow, we went to get drinks, and I spent the entire time trying to get Sacha to answer my texts. I stepped outside to try to call him, and Tip followed. He kissed me before I saw it coming. I immediately jumped away, but apparently, someone had been taking pictures of us at the exact right time. I set Tip straight, but Sacha won't speak to me to let me explain and apologize."

Baylor pushed him toward his car. "Then go now while he's still home. Beg for forgiveness."

"You seriously believe me?"

Baylor's face screwed up in confusion. "Of course I do. You'd never lie to me, but just like you giving Chipper the keys to your place so he could talk me down from my bullshit, I have to call you on yours. I knew you two were dating, but I didn't say anything because I'd never seen either of you so happy. I figured we'd talk about it when you were ready to let me into your bubble. Seriously, I love you both and I can't watch either of you hurt. With Sacha, I do what I can while letting him keep his pride, but he needs you. I think you two genuinely love each other, so don't lose that, okay?"

"You think Sacha loves me?"

For a moment, Baylor stared at him in silence before shaking his head. "I swear I have never met another person as completely blind as you. You never see when people want you. It would be funny if it didn't end up hurting people."

Bandit winced. "I don't ever want to assume."

Baylor swiped his hand across his lips, as if fighting back a smile. He shoved at Bandit's arm. "Go. Don't fuck this up."

Before he got away, Bandit snagged Baylor around the waist and kissed his forehead. "I love you. Thanks for being my friend."

"Forever and always, twin flame, or whatever the fuck that street psychic screamed at us."

Despite the pains in his chest, Bandit chuckled. They were good. Baylor always had his back.

Chapter Eight

Chapter Eight

WITH A DEEP BREATH for courage, Tip jogged up the front steps of the red brick townhouse. He didn't give himself time to change his mind. Tip rang the doorbell. He reached out to push the button a second time when a minute passed. Before he could, the door swung wide, and Tip found himself staring at the most beautiful man he had ever seen. It wasn't Sacha. He had only seen Sacha's picture for a few seconds, but this guy was different. Younger. Sexier. It took Tip a second to catch his breath.

"Hey. Um. Is Sacha home?"

Hatred stared back at him. Whoever this was had obviously seen that picture. Fuck his life.

The guy opened his mouth, and a loud scraping noise filled the air behind him. He turned, leaving the door open enough for Tip to see inside. "Goddamn it, Baba. Why are you dragging that thing out? You can't even get a glass of water alone." He stormed away, leaving the door open.

Tip took it as an invitation and stepped inside. An elderly lady, who was barely skin and bones, dragged a huge black cauldron across the floor, showing a strength he wouldn't have believed.

"I might be old, but the magic from ancient Romani blood runs through the veins thanks to my mother."

Sacha stepped out from a nearby doorway with his gaze locked on the older woman. "What are you doing?"

The woman ignored him and continued her rant. "I can still cook up a mean curse and I'll be damned if any grandson of mine gets cheated on."

"Yeah. He didn't cheat. That was my fault."

Everyone froze. All eyes turned his way.

Tip shifted from foot to foot. He cleared his throat and focused on Sacha. "Sorry. I got your address from Chipper. Everything is entirely my fault. I mistook Bandit's natural kindness for more. When I kissed him, he was horrified and immediately jumped away. He was pretty upset about me ruining what he has with you." Tip couldn't stop. He didn't know why. No one spoke, and he was uncomfortable. The combination had him rambling. "In my defense, I didn't know about you. You haven't been to any games, and Bandit is obviously clueless as hell when someone is hitting on him."

To his surprise, a smile exploded across Sacha's face. "That he is. It took him forever to realize I had been flirting with him for years."

"I didn't realize it. Chipper pointed it out."

Everyone turned toward the door as Bandit appeared with flowers in hand.

Bandit ignored everyone. His gaze never wavered from Sacha. "Can we talk?"

Sacha nodded and stepped back inside the room he'd just appeared from. Bandit stepped around him and followed Sacha inside without acknowledging a single soul. He closed the door behind them.

Tip's gaze slid back toward the man he needed to know more about. "I truly am sorry. I never meant to hurt anyone."

The elderly lady straightened. "Well, Bandit is an irresistible guy. Close the door. Electricity isn't free. Once you've done that, you can carry this cauldron back to the closet. Then I'll leave you with Artem since you're fucking him with your eyes. He could stand to get some."

"*Baba*!" Artem sounded horrified as hell.

A shocked burst of laughter escaped Tip, but he rushed to do as told. No way would he miss an opportunity like this. He might be dumb, but he wasn't that fucking dumb. Tip knew a good thing when he saw it.

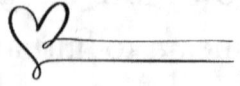

Sacha crossed his arms across his chest, trying to protect his heart as Bandit shut them inside the room. He moved to his bed and sat when his knees shook. Bandit was here. Sacha was weak. He looked tired and beautiful. It wasn't fair. Sacha probably looked like shit. He had spent so much time crying, he felt sick.

"I love you. Please don't break my heart like this."

Of all the things Sacha expected, that wasn't it. To his horror, he burst into tears again.

Bandit was across the room in an instant. He practically threw the flowers on the bedside table before wrapping his arms around Sacha. He smelled so good.

"I'm so sorry. You didn't deserve what I put you through last night. You were busy with your family, and I didn't see what you did with Tip. Tell me what to do. I'll do whatever you need to fix this."

"I feel so ridiculous. You didn't deserve for me to... ugh. I can't remember words."

Bandit kissed his temple and held him tighter. "It's okay. Take a breath. I'm not going anywhere. You have time to work it out in your head."

Damn it. Sacha loved him so much. He didn't know where to start. Bandit was an idiot, blind to his charms. Sacha felt like he was also to blame. He had been the ugly sort of jealous and refused to speak to Bandit.

"Next time, I'll believe in your wisdom when you tell me someone has a thing for me."

A watery laugh burst from Sacha. "It was actually Baba who noticed. She didn't like the way Tip touched her man."

A sexy rumble of laughter came from Bandit's chest. Sacha pressed closer to the sound. His heartbeat gave Sacha the courage and peace he needed.

"I shouldn't have ignored your calls and texts. Your refusal to believe me mixed with my jealousy and I don't know what happened. I've never been in love before. No one told me it would hurt."

Bandit linked fingers with him. "I don't think it's supposed to. I just think I'm dumb."

Sacha's lips found Bandit's throat. He felt Bandit swallow.

"I've never felt this way about anyone else. If I'm failing, I need you to tell me because I can't lose you, Sacha. There's no one else out there for me. I honestly believe part of the reason I was so blind to Tip is because I don't see anyone but you in this way. You're the one I want. Forever."

Sacha's heart couldn't take it. He snagged Bandit's hair and took the kiss he wanted. His feelings poured out and flooded their kiss. In no time, he was on his back with Bandit swinging between touching him everywhere and flattening his palms against the mattress, as if trying to keep them still.

"I'm sorry. You don't deserve to always have me pawing at you. I'd never want you to think that's the only reason I come around."

Gah. He was so sickeningly perfect. Sacha pushed Bandit's shirt up, stealing it. "Paw at me. I love it."

Bandit's hands returned to his body, but he didn't move fast. Sacha was fully aware of every brush of his fingers. He didn't miss the way Bandit slowly stripped him.

Sacha enjoyed the show of Bandit rolling a condom down his length and savored the way his body ached while Bandit lubed and stretched Sacha's asshole.

"I wish you could see what I do when I look at you. You'd never think you're not special again." Sacha meant every word. With his lips swollen, cheeks flushed, and lust burning in his eyes, Bandit was the sexiest vision Sacha had ever encountered.

Bandit's mouth quirked. "That's probably not true. I just think you see something in me no one else does." His eyes turned twice as intense. "And I thank God for it every day." His cock slowly slid inside Sacha, stretching him wide. Bandit stared down at him, openly watching Sacha writhe. "You have no idea how much I longed every day for you to notice me. I would stare and beg the universe for you to look my way." Bandit rocked inside him. "There's been a lot of times in my life when I hated my inability to read people. But you'll never understand how much I resent the years I could've spent with you if I had known we felt the same." He swiped his lips across Sacha's mouth and thrust. "You're the only man I see, and now that I know I have your attention, I can't look away. All I want to do is to be right here." He gently rolled his hips, giving Sacha maximum pleasure while also making tears fill Sacha's eyes.

"I love you." Sacha couldn't hold back the whispered words. They were the truest he had ever spoken.

Bandit's lips skimmed his cheek, moving toward his mouth. "I love you too. Please don't leave me."

A strength Sacha hadn't known he possessed overcame him. "Never." He rolled, pinning Bandit beneath him. Sacha took the pleasure he wanted. Bandit's features turned feral as Sacha bounced on his dick, setting the pace. He visibly strained to hold out long enough for Sacha to come.

"You're so fucking sexy. I want to watch you shake beneath me."

Bandit's expression was fierce as he bared his teeth and spoke with a clenched jaw. "Stop fucking talking, Sacha. I'm about to disappoint the hell out of you."

"You could never disappoint me. Let me watch you lose control."

He saw the moment Bandit lost the battle against himself. His entire body jerked in the sexiest of shows. A loud gasp tore through the room. Satisfaction roared through Sacha. He had done that. No matter how many people sought to steal Bandit, Sacha was the one making his control snap.

The world spun past him. Sacha found himself on his back and his cock in Bandit's mouth. Every thought fled while he strained against the hot suction. Bandit was so fucking talented in everything he did. Sacha scratched at his shoulders and the covers beneath him, trying to cling to any speck of sanity. His hips wouldn't stop lifting, trying to take what he wanted. Bandit never let up. He bobbed fast on Sacha's dick. Tension coiled inside him, tightening by the second. His every muscle tensed. He bit his lip to keep from crying out the way he wanted. Even in his lust, he was hyperaware of his family still outside his room. His body shook as wave after wave washed away his every thought. Pleasure rocked his soul. He saw their future unfold. They were together for every second.

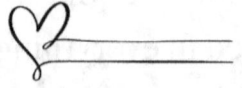

Bandit couldn't stop trailing his fingers up and down the back of Sacha's arm. He loved the way chill bumps formed beneath his touch. With Sacha using his chest as a pillow, he was in heaven, but he still felt like they had so much to talk about. The more he had thought about Tip's accusations, the more Bandit had come to realize he couldn't let Sacha continue to flounder along, barely giving himself a second to breathe. While Sacha had his pride, that trait was killing him under the weight of what more than one man should be forced to handle. Bandit was in the position to make his life easier, and he would, even if he had to go around Sacha to do it.

He opened his mouth while still unsure of how to start.

"I got fired today."

Everything inside Bandit lit with rage. He nearly leapt from the bed in his immediate need to tear into Baylor.

Sacha didn't give his rage time to truly take root. "Well, actually, Baylor has decided to dissolve his business to focus on family. He gave me five years' severance and has already set up thirty specialty cake orders for me to start my own business."

Damn. Bandit kind of wanted to kiss Baylor right on the mouth. "That's awesome, for both of you, honestly. Baylor will never feel secure being away from a child again once they adopt and you should be living your dream. Not his."

He felt Sacha shrug. "Maybe, but working on his dream meant avoiding more responsibilities I don't know how to handle. I didn't have to worry about taxes and overhead. All I had to do with Baylor was my job and collect my salary. Now I have all these things at once and I'm terrified of failing."

Bandit saw his opening. "Last night, when I rejected Tip, he accused me of making you up because you'd never been to a game. I told him you were busy working. He asked why you'd need to do that since you have me."

Sacha went up on one elbow and stared down at him. He looked adorably outraged. "That's ridiculous. Your money is not mine. Of course I'd have to work."

Bandit took a breath, but he refused to break eye contact. "Maybe you don't. I mean, I want you to be able to design your cakes, but I also want you to do so stress free. Art probably doesn't come from a place of panic. I love you. You're mine. Don't go into this thing killing yourself, hoping to make ends meet. Let me take care of you. Come live with me." He could see the sadness rising in Sacha's eyes. He hurried to squash it. "All of you. Baba and Artem too. Let me help you with nursing care and be the extra hand you need. We're partners. Please stop stealing my right to be your rock."

Sacha chewed his bottom lip. The hope in his eyes crushed Bandit's chest because he felt Sacha's denial coming despite his desire. "This is Baba's home. It's the house she bought and lived with her husband until he died. She'll never leave it, and I can't leave her."

Bandit had always thought the three-story townhouse was damn nice for the way Sacha struggled. He got it now. Everyone had left him to pay for a home that wasn't even his. Then the situation was compounded by everyone else's unwillingness to move to someplace more affordable. Everyone had definitely unabashedly dumped a load on Sacha's shoulders.

Luckily, Bandit was determined and shameless once he had his sights set. "Then let me live here. I'd gladly sell my house to stay with you. Just let me in. I want to be your partner in life."

A sweet smile touched Sacha's lips. He plucked at the covers. "I could never ask that of you."

"You're not asking. I'm begging for you to take me in." He sat up and gently rolled Sacha onto his back. Bandit straddled Sacha's body, ensuring he couldn't get away. "Let's do this thing together. I need to know you're waiting in my bed when I get home. When I have a game, I want you there."

Sacha pulled a face. "I doubt Baba would let it go if I went to the game and didn't watch it with her. She's pretty set on the idea that you're ours."

Bandit smiled despite his frustration. "Then let's figure out how to bring Baba to the games. I can hire someone to push her in a wheelchair."

Sacha snorted. "Hell would snow, or whatever that saying is, before Baba sat in a wheelchair. Now, if you want to hire some big, muscular stripper type to carry her everywhere, she'll go wherever you like."

A laugh burst from Bandit. "If that's what it takes." His smile slipped. He needed this. "Please, Sacha. I never want to feel the way I felt last night ever again. I need to know my home is with you. You're drowning in responsibility that I want to share with you. Let me in."

Sacha's heart was in his eyes, and it was beautiful. "Okay."

With one word, Sacha gave Bandit the entire world. A loud *WOOT* escaped him, forcing him to cover his mouth.

Sacha's eyes swam with laughter. "I can't imagine what Baba will have to say about that later."

Bandit settled down, squishing Sacha beneath him. "We could just stay right here forever and never find out."

"Mmm." Sacha's hands ran up Bandit's body. "I like this plan."

Bandit did too. They might never leave this bed again.

Chapter Nine

SACHA WORKED TO PUT himself together to his best. It was the first game of a new season. Last year, they had loved swinging that camera his way for some reason. Bandit had already left. A teammate had picked him up so Bandit could leave with Sacha. It was crazy how Sacha felt as he headed for his bedroom door. Well, Bandit and his bedroom. He saw the man every day damn near all day. They went to bed together each night and woke up beside each other every morning. Still, Sacha couldn't wait to get to him. He wanted to set eyes on Bandit, even if it was only on the field. But damn, he looked fine as fuck on that field.

Sacha stepped out into a world of commotion. Dana looked beyond exasperated, trying to keep Baba in a wheelchair while Artem looked done with all of it. It was forecasted to be a decent temperature outside, but Baba wore her coat. Artem had his shoes on and keys out.

"What's all this?"

Baba quickly sat, as if Sacha would spank her if she didn't behave. "We're going to the game. You took ages to get ready. I'm an old lady. This chair hurts my ass."

Sacha blinked. He didn't even know where the chair had come from. Sacha was equally shocked Baba sat in it at all. "You're all going to the game?"

Baba nodded. "Bandit asked. He bought me a chair and everything. I couldn't say no then, could I? That's rude."

A smile exploded across Sacha's face at the way Baba acted as if she didn't want to go, chair or not. "Okay. Hold on one more second." Sacha darted into Baba's room and grabbed two of her million pillows from the bed. He returned with his haul. "Stand up. You'll be miserable if you try to sit through this game and you're already hurting."

"That's why I didn't want to sit yet. Everyone kept forcing me."

"Nobody forces you to do anything, Baba," Artem grumbled under his breath.

Sacha put a pillow on the seat and another against the back. "Try it now."

Baba sat. She squished her butt around, as if testing it out. A bright smile lit her face.

"Perfect. Now let's go before we miss all that sexy stretching before the game."

With a headshake and a smile, Sacha headed for the door. He hoped the wheelchair fit in Artem's SUV or Sacha didn't know what would happen. Thankfully, the transfer and stashing went smoothly. Everyone was oddly silent during the ride. Sacha was fine with the quiet. He stared out the window and mused over the past year of his life. Bandit had truly swept in and took over. For the first time in a long time, Sacha breathed easier. Bandit could afford extra nursing care and simply having his extra hands made all the difference in the world. Plus, Sacha got to live his dream at his pace, and it was such a fucking relief. It had been the best year of his life. He kind of hated it was already time for a new season, but Bandit loved his career. So Sacha loved it too.

By the time they got settled with Baba and all her snacks at the stadium, Sacha was already exhausted. He truly didn't understand why Baba enjoyed being such a handful all the time. Every time Sacha had sat down, she had sent him to get another snack she had forgotten. Lord, he hoped she didn't plan to be this difficult the entire season.

Artem glanced around, checking out the stadium as if he had never been there. Sacha watched as his gaze landed on the booth. Tip could barely be seen, but Sacha still hid a smile over Artem seeking him out. Tip had taken a job as a sports commentator for the team. Sacha knew Artem always looked at Tip in just a certain way. He had no clue where that was headed, though.

As the stadium filled, Bandit's team jogged out onto the field. Sacha stared at each one until he spotted Bandit. Bandit's head immediately moved his way, as if making sure Sacha had shown. He smiled and waved before moving to warm up. Sacha fought a happy sigh. Bandit was so cute. He was like a little kid searching for his parents in the crowd during a school play. Sacha loved him so much.

Loud music poured through the speakers and the usual pregame shit of giving away prizes and whatnot happened. He lost interest until the game began. Then Sacha was on the edge of his seat. Nearing the end of the game during a dead ball situation, Artem nudged him and pointed toward the big screen above the scoreboard. Sacha's face was there for the world to see. For a moment, he was horrified until he realized what he looked at.

Will you marry me?

Sacha blinked and then blinked again. His mind couldn't absorb what he read. Then

Bandit was there on one knee with an open ring box.

"What do you say?"

Sacha covered his mouth and fell into Bandit's sweaty arms. He didn't care. Happiness choked him. Still, he forced an answer past his lips. He knew Bandit likely didn't have long and probably had only been allotted this time because of how many years he had played for the team.

"Yes. Are you joking? Of course, it's yes."

The crowd roared and Bandit stole a quick kiss before putting the ring on Sacha's finger and disappearing as quickly as he had appeared. He heard Tip talking about congratulations and things of that nature, but Sacha couldn't hear a word through his shock. That had really just happened, and he had never wanted anything more.

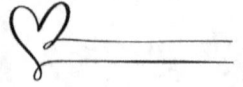

Bandit half expected Sacha to kill him for embarrassing him the second he stepped from the locker room. Instead, he was greeted by one of the hottest kisses he had ever experienced.

He chuckled as he pulled away. "Hello to you too. Where's everyone else?"

"I sent them home. Don't worry. There's a car waiting. I can't believe you did that."

Bandit shuffled Sacha against the wall, crowding his space. "Honestly? Me either. I don't remember half the game because I was so sick with nerves. If you would've said no, it would've been humiliating as fuck, but you deserve a big and public display. You deserve everything." The love that stared back at him made every moment of worry worthwhile. Bandit would never again allow anyone to think he was single. He wanted their relationship as public as possible. Bandit wanted everyone to know Sacha was his.

"I would never humiliate you."

Worry set in without warning. "Fuck. You don't feel cornered, do you? Did I make you feel like you couldn't say no?"

Sacha grabbed his face and covered his mouth in another soul-blazing kiss. "Stop. I definitely want this. I think I would've married you the night Baylor got married if you had been willing."

Bandit chuckled and pressed his forehead against Sacha's. "As crazy as it sounds, I was willing. I think I've always known you were the one for me. There's always been something in my chest when I look at you. It's like I just knew."

Sacha smiled. "Same." The breathless-sounding confession nearly took out Bandit's knees. He knew they should move. Bandit wanted to go home and celebrate properly, but—another thought hit.

Bandit groaned. "I just realized we probably won't get a moment to ourselves until late tonight once we get home. Baba will never let us lock ourselves away."

Sacha took his hand. "I know. That's why I hired a car and got us a hotel room."

Relief poured over Bandit. He let Sacha lead him away like the lovesick puppy he was. "You're perfect."

Sacha's sexy smile flashed his way, and Bandit knew his entire life had led him to this moment. This person. It might have taken them years to finally see each other clearly, but Bandit thought that maybe made them appreciate each other more. No matter the hows or whys, Bandit couldn't wait to spend his life with this man who had stolen him completely. He had never stood this close to fate. The view was amazing.

Keep an eye out for the next Sporting Pride, *Announcing Love*.

About the Author

CHARITY PARKERSON IS AN award-winning and multi-published author with several companies. Born with no filter from her brain to her mouth, she decided to take this odd quirk and insert it in her characters. One of her greatest loves is writing morally gray characters. You'll find them scattered throughout her hundreds of titles.

*Nine-time Readers' Favorite Award Winner

*2015 Passionate Plume Award Finalist

*2013 Reviewers' Choice Award Winner

*2012 ARRA Finalist for Favorite Paranormal Romance

*Five-time winner of The Mistress of the Darkpath

Connect with her online:

*Sign up for her newsletter: https://bit.ly/charityparkersonnewsletter

*Join her readers' group on Facebook: http://bit.ly/CharitysTribe

* Website : https://www.charityparkerson.com

*A list of her social media accounts and giveaways all in one place: http://hy.page/charityparkerson